Please return

The Callisto series by
Jackie French

The Café on Callisto
Space Pirates on Callisto
Vampire Slugs on Callisto

THE CAFÉ ON CALLISTO

JACKIE FRENCH

Illustrated by
Sarah Baron

Catnip
PUBLISHING LTD

To Lewis with love from Aunt Jackie -
never settle for a tasteless tomato.

CATNIP BOOKS
Published by Catnip Publishing Ltd
Islington Business Centre
3-5 Islington High Street
London N1 9LQ

This edition first published 2006
1 3 5 7 9 10 8 6 4 2

First published in Australia in 2001 by Koala Books,
4 Merchant Street, Mascot, Australia 2020

A CIP catalogue record for this book is available
from the British Library

ISBN 10: 1 84647 003 X
ISBN 13: 978 1 84647 003 5

Printed in Poland

www.catnippublishing.co.uk

What's so weird
about a café on Callisto?

What's wrong with living on Earth?

PART ONE

CHAPTER 1

'These are not tomatoes,' muttered Dad, staring at the plate in front of him.

I looked at them. They looked like tomatoes to me. They were bright fire alarm red, just like tomatoes should be. They were round too. They even said '!Tomato!' plainly in yellow on the side – some new form of advertising bioengineering that the technologists had come up with lately. What more did Dad want in a tomato?

'Er ... what are they then, Dad?' I asked.

'Abominations!' yelled Dad. He threw one up in the air and watched as it bounced up and down on the floor. *Boing! Boing! Boing!*

Dad snatched it up on the third bounce.

'Tomatoes should taste of the sun and the earth,' he cried, as he sliced it into quarters, then threw them into the pot along with the frozen, chopped NoSting Onions (even Dad can't get fresh onions any more) and Medi*Chillies (guaranteed extra high in carotene to ward off stomach cancer) and HiFibre 'Mello Yello' Pumpkin. (Dad says that 'Mello Yello' Pumpkin looks like something out of a baby's nappy.)

'Tomatoes should drip with juice when you cut them!' Dad snorted, as he stirred the pan. Even if they weren't 'real' tomatoes in there, those frying veg were starting to smell pretty good to me.

'Tomatoes should have seeds in them and juice and ...'

'Why should tomatoes have seeds?' I asked. I really wanted to know. Who cares about seeds? After all, we weren't going to plant them – not down here, twenty-five floors below ground level.

Dad and I do have a garden, of course, but it's mostly just SmogBush and Ultra!Grass since our sector's ventilator cleaning system broke down three years ago. Ventilator Management *said* they'd fixed it (huh!), but even Dad's bean sprouts turn yellow now. The air also smells like my Foot

Flaks after a day in virtual gym. I've sort of got used to the pong, but I don't suppose plants can.

'Because the flavour's in the tomato juice around the seeds!' Dad exclaimed, waving his favourite chopping knife in the air. 'Without seeds you don't have flavour! Tomatoes should smell of sunlight and the earth, not some hydroponic factory! They should ooze sweetness on your tongue!'

My dad gets carried away about food sometimes. Okay, I admit it, most of the time. Cooking was Dad's life, except for me, and I suppose, Mum when she was alive – and from what Dad has said Mum was passionate about food too.

Mum and Dad met in Dad's café. It was above ground in those days, before the Clearances. Mum and Dad weren't forced to shift twenty-five floors down here out of the ultraviolet till just after I was born.

Anyway, Dad'd just made spaghetti with minced chicken meatballs and ricotta and basil (the old-fashioned stuff, not hydroponic – Dad had a real garden then) and Mum took one sniff of that oozing garlic herby richness then looked into Dad's eyes ... and I was born ten months later, or at least that's the way Dad tells it.

Mum and Dad ran the café together for six

years, just them and it and me, till Mum was killed in the water riots back in '55. And then it was just Dad and me. And the café of course.

Not that I'm much of a cook – to be honest I think cooking is totally bureaucratic, though I'm a *really* keen eater. My job was the repairs; I was pretty good at them too. Don't ever let anyone kid you that you have to be grown up to change a ventilator filter, or to open the lid of Floor 25's waste disposal duct. (You should have *seen* the stuff they had down there! It was totally supanova gruesome! At least it was till Dad hauled me out of there.)

Dad poured stock into the pot, so all the steam hooshed up, all damp and fragrant and yummy, and my nose started to send 'time to eat' messages to my stomach.

Dad's menu said tomato and pumpkin soup tonight, and when his menu said tomato and pumpkin soup that's exactly what it was made of – we were the last café in the whole of our sector to use fresh food instead of flavour tablets. (You should have heard the body corporate complain about our garbage.)

Dad looked out the window broodingly while I tried to tell my stomach it's not polite to gurgle.

It wasn't a real window of course – not twenty-five floors underground – but it was a pretty view anyway. It looked just like this mid-20th century garden with a lemon tree bursting with fat yellow fruit and little brown birds pecking at the corn. Mum had given it to Dad for their second wedding anniversary and you could program it to display over a dozen different patterns – rain and wind and lemon blossom or ripe fruit or even a night setting with an owl hunting mice above the corn.

Dad seemed to be looking out Mum's window a lot lately.

'That's what tomatoes should be like,' said Dad, still staring out the window.

'But, Dad,' I said reasonably (it's hard to get parents to be rational sometimes), 'there aren't any tomatoes out the window.'

Dad ignored me. 'Food should be grown in sunlight, not under ArtiGlo. It should taste of soil, not nutrient solution. You should be able to touch the buds, smell it growing, run your fingers through the soil ...'

'Hey, Dad, guess what happened at school today?' I tried to change the subject. 'Mrs Hobbins forgot to program in our lunch break, so we worked right through! She is totally bureaucratic sometimes! I'm really starving! Then, this afternoon, an advertisement broke away from its matrix and kept dancing through the classroom – it was an ad for shoes or something, and it had these tapdancing gorillas and one of them jumped right on my ...'

Dad shook his head. 'This isn't the life you should be leading, Sam.'

'I'm okay,' I said. 'It was pretty funny. I had this dancing gorilla sticking out of my ...'

'No, you're not okay,' said Dad. 'When was the last time you saw sunlight?'

'I see sunlight lots.' I racked my brains. 'Last Christmas, remember? You took me out to breakfast in a park with a window and there was genuine water outside and everything ...'

'You've never even eaten a strawberry straight from the bush! Or swum in water that's touched the earth.'

'Dad, there's a swimming pool at school! It's

thirty-six levels down below, right at the bottom, so of course it's touching the earth ...'

It was as though he hadn't heard me. Parents don't really listen much, I've decided, not when they've got something on their minds. Sometimes I wish you could reprogram parents too ...

'You're just like the tomatoes, Sam. Can't you see?'

'Huh?' I said. 'Me?'

I may not be totally supanova gorgeous, but I don't look like a tomato! Not the last time I looked in a mirror anyway.

'Tomatoes taste of where they're grown,' said Dad earnestly. 'It's the same with people. Kids shouldn't have to grow up twenty-five floors underground, with advertisements dancing along the corridors and cluttering up their school space. If you take away the sunlight and the trees and space from kids, you take away something else.'

'Like what?' I asked.

Dad shook his head. 'Something I don't have a name for. A tomato loses taste and piquancy. A person loses ... well ... part of what makes us human maybe.'

Dad peered out Mum's window again. A small brown bird was pecking at a fallen lemon. In a few minutes it'd fly back up into the tree and lift its head and yell a song up to the sky. I'd seen it a million times by now but I still liked it.

When I looked back Dad was staring at me.

'We had plans, your mother and I. One day we'd take you to the stars. To another planet. Somewhere where the sun still shines, where tomatoes smell like tomatoes and you can hear the rain on the leaves.'

'It wouldn't be our sun out there among the stars,' I said practically, but Dad wasn't listening.

'But then your mother died and somehow ...' Dad shifted his shoulders back. 'Somehow, Samdolyn,' he said, 'somehow we have to get off Earth.'

CHAPTER 2

I suppose if some fathers said anything like that their kids'd go into shock or something. Not me though. I mean, how is a cook like Dad ever going to take his daughter to the stars?

Dad's not a mining engineer or a temporal navigator or even a certified Basics teacher – none of the required jobs for planetary colonisation. Dad couldn't even get a job as a cook on a spaceship – all they serve is spacegloop anyway – and if you can't get a specialist space job, the only other way is to win the space lottery.

We had as much chance of winning as flying up the ventilator shaft – and I don't mean pretending to with those crummy wings you hire in the virtuals either.

There was just one other way to get to the stars of course. That was if someone already out there wanted to come back. It was known as the 'Earthright Principle' – those who were born on Earth always had the right to a place here. If you found someone willing to take your place on Earth, you could take theirs out in the stars.

Some chance!

Which was why I wasn't expecting to find an open spacesak half-filled with kitchen knives and whisks and other cooking junk in the security hall by the front door three weeks later.

'Hey, Dad!' I yelled, as I dumped my school bag by the swing doors leading into the kitchen. 'What's going on? There's a sign in the lift saying "Café closed till further notice" and what's that spacesak doing ...?'

'Shh,' said Dad. 'I'm creating.'

I shut up then, because I could see what he was cooking. I could smell it too – that lovely mix of browning meat and sizzling onions, fresh chopped lettuce ...

My dad is the most inspired hamburger maker in the galaxy – you ask any of my friends if I'm biased or not, and they'll tell you.

First, he mixes herbs and barbecue sauce and stuff like that into the meat patties, and fries the onions till they're golden while the patties are browning. Then he bakes two !Tomato! halves until they're sort of leathery outside but still juicy inside and dusts them with fresh New!Thyme.

Next, he just slightly warms chopped Fresha!Lettuce and three slices of pickled beetroot (and I don't mean from a can – not Dad), while he warms up six slices of bread – without crusts (Dad says crusts ruin a hamburger).

Finally, he puts the whole lot together with more barbecue sauce and, when you take a bite, the meat oozes one way and the onions ooze another and barbecue sauce drips all down your front and then the first bite wriggles down your throat and your stomach says 'ahhhh!' and you *know* you've eaten something wonderful.

There was no way I was going to interrupt him till he'd finished.

Well, anyway, when me and that hamburger were one contented flesh and Dad was sitting down at the kitchen table opposite me with a cup of black tea (for someone who likes cooking as much as Dad does, he doesn't really eat much; sometimes I think some people are born fabulous cooks like him and some people are born fabulous eaters like me) I finally asked, 'Hey, Dad, what's with the spacesak in the security hall?'

Dad just beamed. He didn't say anything. He

just looked at me with stars (yes, real ones) in his eyes, and for the first time in ages I felt that he was really looking at the future too, not just at the past or a window that wasn't really there.

'Dad ... Dad, you don't mean ...?'

Dad nodded slowly. His grin got wider, then wider still. I mean it – really wider, as if he should have been dancing round the kitchen but was saving his dancing till later ...

'We're off to the stars!' said Dad.

'But how ... ?'

'We're going to Callisto 4,' he said, and there was so much joy in his voice that I didn't care what he was about to say – anything that made Dad look like that had to be good.

'It's an exchange – a once-in-a-lifetime chance, Sam. A once-in-ten-lifetimes chance! A bloke on Callisto 4 has a café. It's the only café on the entire planet, but he's homesick. He wants to exchange his café on Callisto for one here on Earth. And he advertised this morning and I was on the Net just as it came in and was the first to reply and this afternoon approval for the swap came through!'

I blinked. 'Er, great, Dad,' I said. 'Just one question?'

'What, Sam?' beamed Dad.

'Where the heck is Callisto 4?'

CHAPTER 3

I don't suppose you've heard of Callisto 4 either. No, it's not the moon Callisto that orbits Jupiter in our solar system. Callisto is a sun too, a gazillion light years from Earth, and Callisto 4 is the fourth planet away from that sun. All the other planets circling Callisto are either too hot or too cold for humans, but Callisto 4 is like Earth used to be, just about perfect.

That's what Dad said anyway, and so did the encyclopaedia when I dialled it up. I find it's a good idea to check Dad's facts sometimes – he gets a bit vague about things, unless you can cook them or serve them up in the café.

But it looked like Dad was right on target this time. Don't get me wrong, Callisto isn't one of the great space colonies. You don't go out there to make your fortune mining Betelgeuseum like on Betelgeuse 11, or farming a million wildebeeste like on Centauri 2/3. It hasn't even had any really major disasters either, like the flesh-eating slime mould on Morganworld or the zombie virus on Tempora 19.

Callisto was settled right at the beginning of colonisation by an organic gardening group who raised their own funds to set up the colony themselves. They wanted to use Callisto as a sort of seed bank for all the lost plant varieties on Earth. Nowadays, we take it for granted that everything is genetically engineered – the one best variety of apple or orange or tomato. It's more productive, isn't it, to use only the biggest and best-selling crop of everything?

It's only nostalgia freaks like Dad who long for the way plants used to be. Dad says the 'best' varieties aren't really the best at all. Dad and the people of Callisto 4.

Callisto 4 didn't have much in the way of mineral reserves or gemstones or plants for pharmaceuticals. What it did have was soil that seemed to have been waiting for Earth plants for the last 2 billion years. Things grew abundantly on Callisto 4 – at least that's what the library bank told me when I looked it up.

'Dad?'

'Mmmm?' Dad was already dreaming of the things he'd cook on Callisto.

'What sort of a nullbrain bureaucrat would want to give up a café on Callisto for our place here on Earth?'

'Mmm? I thought I told you, honey. He's homesick.'

'Homesick for ventilator air and engineered !Tomatoes!?'

Dad blinked. For the first time he seemed to be listening to what I was saying. 'Look, Sam, people are different. If the whole world hated !Tomatoes! and Fresha!Lettuce people would rise up in protest. But they don't! Most people on Earth don't care about how they live or what they eat.'

'But this guy can't be like that! If he didn't like cooking and old-fashioned real food and stuff, he wouldn't have gone to Callisto! Dad, it's just too easy. There has to be a catch! Maybe the café's a dump.'

Dad shook his head.

'There were registered photos of it on the Net,' he said. 'It's small but it's pretty ...'

'Maybe it's going broke?'

Dad laughed. 'Honey, it's the only café on Callisto, the place where people love their food most in the universe! How could it be going broke?'

'I don't know. It's just ...'

Dad looked at me seriously, 'Sam, it'll be a good life out there. I promise. But if you really don't want to go ...'

I hesitated. You know, it's funny, I'd never really considered whether I wanted to go or not. I just assumed we *were* going, following Dad's dream.

I looked around the kitchen I'd known all the life I could remember – the giant frying pan on the wall, the banks of dishwashers, the blackened grill, the old smells of frying spices and fresh cakes. I bet some of those smells were so old they might have been from meals that Dad cooked for Mum, all those years ago. I'd miss it all, but any kitchen that had Dad in it – and his cooking – I'd be happy in as well.

I'd be leaving my friends too, of course; okay that was a blow, but there'd be kids on Callisto 4 as well. I looked at Mum's window. A butterfly was hovering over a tassel of corn. It landed as I watched.

'Dad, can we take Mum's window?'

'We won't need an artificial window on Callisto ...' began Dad. Then he stopped. He looked at the window too. The butterfly had laid her eggs now and was hovering between the bright green stems, just as she had a hundred thousand times since I was a baby.

'Yes,' he said finally. 'We'll take the window.'

What's so dull about space travel?

PART TWO

CHAPTER 4

I got the feeling something was wrong the first day out.

I said goodbye to Earth through the viewpad (there's only one on the entire ship and they don't leave it open all the time – a problem with radiation shielding or something). I suppose I should have felt sad or nostalgic or something, but I didn't. Earth just looked like a big smudgy balloon that someone had left behind. It didn't even look like a place where people lived and walked, much less anywhere I'd known.

I felt sadder leaving our garden behind if you want to know the truth. That was something I really did love, even if it was just SmogBush and Ultra!Grass and the smell of dead feet from the ventilator shaft.

I felt sorry about leaving my friends, too, but nowadays on Earth you don't actually *see* your friends much. Why go to the movies with someone when you can both see it through the Link at home? That way you don't have to worry about corridor security checks and sector passports and all that stuff.

So you Net with them instead and discuss the movie that way and miss out on all the bureaucratic red tape of actually travelling from one place to another. Even school is just a Link site for the kids in our corridor and most of our customers in the café were from Floor 25 as well. I had really good friends, but somehow I had the feeling it wasn't the same as having friends would have been when Dad was young.

I'd expected our cabin to be small, but I didn't know it was going to be this small.

On the shuttle from Earth to the spaceship it's the weight of everything that counts, because it has to be lifted off Earth; but up in space you're limited by size. So on the spaceship you can only take what you can fit into your cabin and, let me tell you, after Dad had crammed in his precious copper-bottomed saucepans and cooking knives and whisks *and* about two thousand recipe discs, there wasn't much room for either of us.

Zero G is a bore after you've been sick a couple of times ... especially since when you vomit in free fall it flies all over the place and you have to zoom after it with a net. Going grunge-hunting with a vomit net is a great way to make you decide you'll never be spacesick again.

Free fall is a bore after the first few hours too. All the passenger sections of the spaceships are free fall – we weren't going to be in space long enough for zero G to affect our bones or anything much. The ship did have partial gravity in the crew's quarters.

You don't even feel the ship move in space, except for the transtemporal surges as the ship swallowed up great gulps of time. And there's nothing to see out the window either, partly because there aren't any windows, but also because once you're under way all you'd see outside anyway would be a grey time-blur.

That's because you don't actually travel in space nowadays, the ship eats time instead – and if you want more detail than that don't ask me. I *hate* that sort of stuff at school. Transtemporal surges feel like nothing on Earth – well, of course they would – and you wish that you're dead, but you're not.

For lack of anything else to do, I read all the instructions on the wall monitor three times, about where to grab a spacesuit if a meteorite ploughed into us or if we got caught in a radiation storm. The most important bit was what times we were expected in the dining room for meals. Dad left all that to me of course – he was too excited to do anything except plan menus.

So, promptly at three hoots, we hauled ourselves down the corridor (And I do mean hauled – you grab the rail and pull. How else do you think you get along in zero G? Flutter your fairy wings? Even fairy wings need air, buster.) to this tiny grey tin can that was supposed to be the dining room.

Dining room? It made our café look like a fairy palace!

I should have guessed something was wrong when there was no dining table. Just these rows of seats with cords dangling down and nozzles on the ends of the cords.

'Er, excuse me?' I tapped a steward on the shoulder ... well, I tried to tap him on the shoulder but he was pulling himself along from handles on the ceiling as if he'd been born floating in zero G, so I ended up tapping his foot instead.

The steward glanced down at me and smiled like adults do when they want other adults to think how kind and polite they are to kids, when really they'd be happy to see us bunged into rubbish bins and not let out till we were 18. 'Yes, dear?' he said.

I hate people who call me dear.

'What are those nozzles for?'

'That's what you suck your dinner through, dear,' he said. 'Otherwise it would float all over the place. Tonight, it's roast lamb, roast pumpkin, mashed potatoes, peas, ice-cream and strawberries.'

There was no way a nice slice of roast lamb was going to fit through that tube. 'But ...' I began, but the steward had hauled his way across the room and was gone.

So Dad and I sat down on our chairs and I took a hesitant suck at my nozzle. The steward was right. It *was* roast lamb, roast pumpkin, mashed potatoes, peas, ice-cream and strawberry jelly – all mashed up together into this sort of spacegloop.

It made me really, really determined not to be spacesick again. If Dad's triple-decker cheese and mango pickle, cheese and lettuce and cheese and banana and coconut sandwiches had smelt bad turned into spacesick, I'd hate to think what spacegloop would be like.

I glanced over at Dad. I half expected him to leap to his feet and demand that we put in at Mars or somewhere else impossible and pick up a pineapple pizza or a roast chicken and green salad with avocado dressing; but even spacegloop couldn't put a dent in Dad's grin. It was as if it were heat-sealed to his face.

If Dad could eat spacegloop so could I! I shut my eyes and sucked on my nozzle and swallowed my gloop and tried to dream of all the great meals Dad had cooked me back on Earth, and the even more wonderful food I'd be able to get my fangs into on Callisto.

Dad was still dutifully sucking when I'd finished *(yeerk!)*, so I looked around at the other passengers instead.

I knew that just about all of them were going further than us to places people had actually heard of, like NewNewZealand or that new mining colony where everyone is getting rich. Most of them were pretty elderly too, Dad's age or even older. There was just one kid my age in the entire room. He looked like he didn't think much of spacegloop either.

I was just trying to catch his eye when Dad hung up his nozzle and started talking to this *really* elderly couple called Goodsoil who had the gloop tubes next to ours. Turns out they were going back to Callisto after a holiday on Earth, and the kid was their grandson.

Well, in no time flat, Dad and this pair were talking about food – sponge cakes to be precise. Seems this woman's family had been making sponge cakes right back in the Stone Age, and their recipe had been getting better ever since.

'Of course,' Mrs Goodsoil was saying, 'you need perfect eggs to make the perfect sponge cake! Now some people will tell you to use duck eggs, but you know what my secret is?'

Dad shook his head eagerly.

'Really *fresh* eggs,' said Mrs Goodsoil. 'And when I say fresh, I mean no more than two hours old! And they have to be free-range eggs too, with exactly the right kind of food for the chickens.'

'Walnuts and hazelnuts and avocados,' said Mr Goodsoil. 'That's what we have in our orchard. Can't go past nuts and avocados as chook food.'

'I'm sure you're right!' said Dad.

His grin was even wider if possible. 'Do you find it best to sweeten the cream on a sponge cake and serve it with a sour jam like wild cherry? Or do you think plain cream is nicest with a sweet jam?'

Mr and Mrs Goodsoil beamed at him. 'Now in *my* experience ...' said Mr Goodsoil.

'My husband makes all the jam in our family,' interrupted Mrs Goodsoil. 'You should just taste his fig jelly!'

I left them to it. 'Hi,' I said to the boy on the other side of them. 'My name's Sam.'

'I'm Ham,' said the boy. 'Errk, did you taste that tube stuff? I thought it was bad on the way out but it's even worse this time. I can't wait to get home.'

'Have you always lived on Callisto?' I asked.

'Sure,' said Ham.

I grabbed one of the handles in the wall and hauled myself over next to him. This was great! I could really find out about Callisto now. Not to mention having someone to realtalk with during the voyage. 'What's it like?' I demanded.

Ham grinned. 'That's like saying "What's Earth like?" Callisto's a really big planet, just like Earth. Some bits are hot and some bits are cold and ...'

'What's the bit where you live like?'

'Oh, great. It's by the Inland Sea. My parents have a fishing boat. You going anywhere near there?'

I shook my head. It would have been nice to know at least one person when we landed.

'I think we're going right around the other side of the planet,' I said. 'Hey, I hope you don't think I'm rude or anything, but how did you afford to have a holiday on Earth? I thought no one got really rich on Callisto.'

'Sure,' said Ham. 'Just like no one's poor either. Food grows easily on Callisto and there's lots of timber for houses and stuff too, so you don't need much money to live really well. But Callisto doesn't produce anything that Earth really needs, except good food of course, so no one makes squillions of dollars. No, Grandma is President of the Fish Cooperative. We're going to trade mudfish to Earth.'

'It must be great-tasting fish to be worth carting all the way to Earth,' I said.

Ham shook his head. 'Nope. Mudfish tastes like mud. But it's got this substance in its skin and bones that helps to make really hard plastics. But that's Earth for you. They'd rather have plastic than good food.' He looked guilty suddenly. 'Hey, I didn't mean to insult your planet or anything.'

'That's okay,' I said. 'I don't suppose Earth's my planet anymore. Dad and I are going to settle on Callisto.'

'Really!' Ham grinned. 'You wait till you taste Callisto fish! I like flattails best. They're so sweet they just need frying in a little butter with maybe a touch of orange juice and pepper. The flesh just flakes away when you plunge a fork into it ...'

It looked like Dad had been right for once about people from Callisto loving their food. It was time for me to leave.

The next time I saw him I asked, 'So did the Fish Coop pay for your grandmother to go to Earth?'

'What? Oh yeah, and that meant Grandpop and I could go too, because it doesn't cost much if you share the same cabin, just the shuttle fare and food and that. So I got to have a holiday on Earth.'

'Wow!'

'Well, yeah,' said Ham unenthusiastically. 'Earth was okay, I suppose. It just wasn't what I expected.'

'What did you expect?'

'Well, you know, like in all the books and on the Net ... pirates and lions and tigers in the jungles. I thought maybe we'd ride on elephants and stuff like that.'

'There haven't been any elephants on Earth for years,' I told him loftily. 'No pirates either.'

'Yeah, I know that now,' said Ham gloomily. 'Just shows you shouldn't go trusting stuff on the Net.'

'Uh, yeah ...' I said. It suddenly dawned on me that all my knowledge of Callisto came from books and the Net too.

Maybe I was as out of date about Callisto as Ham had been about Earth.

Maybe all the wonderful vegetables and fruit trees had died last century ... but, no, the Goodsoils had fruit trees.

Perhaps there'd been a flesh-eating space plague though, or an asteroid had hit them and caused a century-long winter, or ...

But before I could think of a way to tactfully ask if there'd been any erupting volcanoes, invasions of vampire bats or other recent disasters on Callisto, Ham was asking me: 'What are you and your dad going to do on Callisto?'

'We're going to run a café,' I said proudly.

Ham blinked. 'Huh? Did you say café?'

'Yeah, I did.'

'A café? You mean it?'

'Sure. My dad's a really great cook, and ...'

'A café on Callisto!'

'Yeah, we had one on Earth and ...'

I stopped. Ham had started to snigger. He sort of chortled, then he gurgled and guffawed.

I stared at him, bewildered. I hadn't said anything funny – had I? Maybe he'd just remembered a joke or something ...

'Garffle gawffle gawffle!' snickered Ham. Finally he laughed so hard he fell off his seat.

Mrs Goodsoil looked at me strangely, as though wondering what sort of spell I'd put on her grandson. 'Oh, is that the time?' she said. 'They'll need the dining room for the next sitting soon. Come on Ham. Ham! Ham!'

Ham picked himself up, still giggling. He staggered out after his grandparents. Just as they went out the door he looked back at me, and started laughing all over again. I could hear his chuckles all the way down the corridor.

Dad stared after them. 'What was that all about?' he demanded.

'Search me,' I said. 'I just told him we were going to run a café on Callisto and he went all weird. Maybe he's mental or something.'

'Could be,' said Dad. 'Maybe that's why they took the poor boy to Earth, to see if the Earth doctors could do anything for him.'

'Yeah, maybe,' I said dubiously.

But he'd seemed normal enough right up until I'd told him about our café ...

There was nothing funny about a café on Callisto.

Was there?

Well, that was about the social highlight of our trip. The Goodsoils avoided *us* after that, as though it was us who were weird. Every time I'd look across the dining room Ham would be looking back at me, and every time our eyes met he'd start laughing again.

It got really embarrassing.

In fact it got so bad that Dad and I changed our meal time to another slot.

Dad spent most of the voyage planning his menus and updating his recipe index and muttering about topping meringues with real cream and raspberry purée and how he'd be able to taste *real* tomatoes once again, and I spent my time exploring.

Not that there's much to explore on a spaceship – not the bits they let the passengers explore anyway. I did try to slip down to the engine room and the temporal function centre, but every time I got near some steward always just happened by.

That didn't leave much else to explore, except the air conditioning ducts. Did you know that air conditioning ducts lead everywhere on a spaceship – even down to the engine room and temporal function centre? All I had to do was get into one of the ducts and I'd be able to go anywhere.

If we'd been back on Earth in full gravity it would have been a cinch – I'm a whizz with a screwdriver. But even a simple task such as unscrewing things is difficult in zero G when your ankles are drifting up above your head and you tend to float back down the corridor if you're not hanging onto something. Besides, whoever installed these ducts did their best to make them passenger-proof.

Well, I'd *almost* worked out how it all went together when this steward came drifting along. It wasn't the snotty one who called me 'dear'. This one was younger. I got the feeling he really saw me, if you know what I mean, not just registered 'alien approaching' on his kid alert.

You could tell he was used to space – he just pushed against the floor/wall/ceiling (you try telling which is which on a spaceship) with his fingertips every so often, instead of hauling arm over arm on the handholds like us passengers.

I smiled at him innocently (I'm good at that). 'Just doing my warm-up exercises out here in the corridor,' I said. 'It's so cramped in the cabin.'

He gave me that 'Oh yeah, kid' sort of look. 'Which is your cabin?' he asked.

'22 V deck.'

'Oh yes, you're ...' he looked at his handheld terminal, 'Samdolyn Major, travelling with her father, Vince Major.'

'That's us,' I said.

He was still looking suspiciously at where I'd been examining the air duct cover, so I said (just to distract him), 'We're off to run a café on Callisto 4'.

The steward stared. He didn't say anything for a full deciminute.

Then he smiled. It was a polite steward-type 'how nice for you' smile – at first anyway. But his grin just got bigger and bigger, as though he couldn't help it, and then a giggle popped out and then another, and finally he gave this great bark of laughter and started holding his sides, so he started to drift down the corridor.

He was still chortling as he sailed around the curve of the passageway and drifted out of sight.

'Dad?'

'Mmm?' Dad was tethered to the driftquilt just above me, nearly asleep.

'What do you really know about this café we're going to?'

'Mmmm – you know as much as I do. Go to sleep, Sam.'

'But, Dad ...'

'Go to sleep. You've seen the photos. It looks like a great place. Plenty of seating, a nice house attached. The only café on the entire planet has to be a moneyspinner.'

'But, Dad, why aren't there more cafés on Callisto if everyone loves food so much?'

'Running a café is more than good cooking. You need to be able to balance a menu, do the books, work out the cost effectiveness, timetable the meals in the dinner rush ...' Dad's voice trailed off and the snores began.

'But, Dad ...'

More snores. I lay there suspended in my driftquilt and pondered.

Something was wrong. Something had to be wrong. No one gave up paradise just because they were homesick for Earth. Maybe there was something really wrong with Callisto that no one had mentioned? Maybe it stank or there were clouds of biting insects or everyone was really unfriendly?

Earthquakes maybe? Poisonous gas? Venomous snakes the size of your finger that darted out of crevices and savaged your ankles? A really terrible insanity virus that made people laugh all the time? Space vampires ...?

But surely there'd be *some* reference somewhere on the Net if there was anything like that. The colonies have a 'full disclosure' policy. Colonies simply can't keep secrets.

It *looked* all right. The perfect planet, a population of food fanatics, and us with the only café in the world. It couldn't fail?

Could it?

CHAPTER 5

The rest of the trip was okay. Boring, but okay. Three months in space sounds exciting, but after all, what is space? Just space: just nothing. And that just about says it all.

Like I said, nothing much happened for the whole three months we were in space. I finally got that air duct cover off in our third last week out, but another steward found me just as I was crawling up inside.

I tried to tell him I was only trying to catch my pet mouse, but he just gave me a dirty look and said, 'There is no pet mouse listed on the ship's manifest. You come with me, young lady.'

So the captain had one of those adult-to-adult conversations with Dad and then she confined me to the cabin for the rest of the voyage, except for those so-called meals (yuk!). Talk about totally bureaucratic!

I spent the prison time floating about and reading – luckily microdiscs don't take up much space – and dreaming about Callisto 4 and wondering if the guy who was swapping cafés with us was suspended in his cabin too, dreaming about Earth.

Or was he sighing in relief that he'd finally escaped the space vampires?

What's so scary
about starting again in a new place?

PART THREE

CHAPTER 6

The last week of the trip they finally gave us passengers some gravity, so that we could find out where our muscles had got to again.

I spent most of my time exercising – the vid in each cabin gives you a full exercise program – and making sure Dad did his too. He wasn't going to be much use in the restaurant if he was too weak to stand up, was he? You can get really flabby in three months of zero G.

Docking was long and totally bureaucratic. This official came up and examined our papers. (What did he think – that someone had sneaked on board in deep space when no one was looking? He must have known already who we were and why we were here.)

We filled out more papers and *more* papers and then they loaded us into this space ferry buggy thing, which bounced us around and around and didn't even have any windows so that we could see where we were going. Finally, it landed on Callisto at this big terminal, which looked just like any other terminal anywhere in the universe, and all you could smell was airconditioning and that grey carpet which I reckon is the same all over the universe too.

I didn't get spacesick, mostly because I was too scared.

It hadn't really struck me till now that Callisto was going to be *different!* Even if it didn't have space vampires, or a laughing virus, or a great hole where some meteor had crashed, it was going to be stranger than anything I'd ever known. A whole different planet, with no corridors or levels – just *space* and sky and sun and trees that you could touch and, even worse, new people.

Worst of all, these new people would be used to sun and sky and other weird stuff and would probably think me strange instead.

Maybe Dad was right about sunlight and soil making things different. Maybe these new people would look at me the way Dad looked at !Tomatoes! back home ...

So, anyway, we all had to stand on this great conveyor belt that took us down a whole corridor of showers, with our clothes on and all, and then along another corridor of heated superdry air that almost instantly dried us.

Maybe it was for disinfection or something, but after three months of trying to wash in a blob of water that drifted slowly all over the cabin until you tried to dab your washer in it, when it sped away as if it had a mind of its own, it felt pretty good to be clean. Luckily I'd pulled my hair back in a ponytail, so it wasn't a complete mess.

Then our luggage was inspected and we were inspected *again*, and Dad put his fingerprint on three million terminals (they didn't even ask for mine *once*, just because I'm a kid, which I thought was totally bureaucratic). How did they know I was really me without my fingerprint? Dad could have smuggled in anyone and said she was his daughter. I could have been an intergalactic psychopath or a certified space zombie for all the people on Callisto knew, but no one ever thinks kids can be anything interesting.

Then they pointed us down this great grey corridor and along we went, pushing our luggage trolleys, with about fourteen others who were getting off at Callisto (I made sure I kept right away from the Goodsoils). Suddenly, I could smell something strange, a zillion scents all put together, like nothing I'd ever smelt before but sort of good ... and there we were in this gigantic room.

I mean it was *big!* It was the biggest room I'd ever been in and it was full of this really cool yellow light, which I suddenly realised was sunlight! Can you imagine ... light from a great big burning globe in the sky, and not from a light tube at all!

And the walls weren't grey at all, but all sorts of wood colours, and somehow I just knew it was real wood too! Only millionaires have genuine wood now on Earth, and here we were surrounded by it!

The room was full of people. At first glance they looked like normal humans – no two heads or tails or anything like that. It was only when my eyes got used to all the space and the sunlight that I noticed that they looked sort of weird too.

For a start, they were all dressed in these really bright colours. No one wears colours like that on Earth, there's just not enough space to cope with bright colours – you'd faint in the glare.

There was something else too, something hard to put your finger on at first. Then I realised what it was.

All the people were *big*, just like the room. Not fat, though there were a couple of tubby ones. It was as if somehow, with all the space and sunlight on Callisto, people here had grown as tall and big-boned as any humans could without being re-engineered. I suppose they just looked really healthy.

What with the size of everything and the bright colours, it was all pretty overwhelming.

Then I saw the food.

CHAPTER 7

I was brought up in a café. I'm used to food. Food and I are really good friends. If you'd asked me a year ago, I'd have said that I couldn't ever be surprised by food. But even I had never seen food like this before.

Tables decorated with long bright tablecloths creaked under all sorts of food – steaming casseroles on tiny burners, platters of pastries with flaky brown tops, and cakes with chocolate icing, yellow icing, raspberry icing, green pistachio icing, or oozing cream and strawberry jam, all crammed together like a giant cityscape, all up and down and around.

There were baskets of fruit on the ground – some of which looked sort of familiar, but there were also many varieties I was sure I'd never even seen before.

There were giant platters of cut fruit, watermelon beaded with drops of moisture that glistened like tiny juicy diamonds, sliced bananas, oranges cut into flower shapes, dark grapes that looked like they were covered in black velvet ...

The whole room smelt of food – the harsh rich scent of pineapple, the hot flour smell of bread fresh from the oven, and a million other smells that my nose had never met before but was pretty sure it liked!

And everyone seemed to be holding a plate of lamingtons or moist applecake or steaming scones or fruit tarts or pastries with their spicy meat or vegie fillings bursting out of them. One woman even had a great big pile of fruit on her *head*, except when I looked again I saw it was a hat.

And everyone was looking at us and time sort of stood still while they looked at us and we looked at them.

Then suddenly this giant woman galloped towards us – she wore this bright red thing that looked like a carpet embroidered with flowers draped over most of her – and she pressed enormous empty plates into our hands and kissed both my cheeks then Dad's cheeks.

'Welcome to Callisto!' she cried, and before we knew it she'd piled these tarts onto our plates and was beaming at us.

'Almond pastry,' she whispered to Dad. 'I make it with extra eggwhites. It's my secret recipe.' (It didn't seem like all that big a secret if she was telling us all about it, I thought.) 'And the raspberries are from our garden – they were a variety first grown for the King of France in 1560 – and you must try ...'

A small man grabbed my elbow. He was skinny all over except for his stomach, which bulged like a frog's.

'I know what you'd like,' he announced. 'Lamingtons. No, ice-cream! Delicious fresh ice-cream! All children like ice-cream, don't they? I make my ice-cream from true Jersey cream – you just don't get the richness from other cows like Alderneys or Friesians. What flavour do you like? There's mango, crushed strawberry – they're genuine alpine strawberries, tiny as a fingernail and sweet as honey – or there's coconut and lemon, chocolate and orange, rose petal, passionfruit ...'

I looked across at Dad. The fat woman was still telling him all about her pastry and Dad was munching it, with a sort of glazed look in his eyes, and getting crumbs all down his shirt, while another woman ladled some sort of green and brown curry onto his plate and another handed him cucumber salad and tomato relish and yet another offered a plate of spiced beans and nuts.

Well, I reckoned there and then I didn't have to worry about people on Callisto not being friendly. They were friendly like octopuses. If they'd been any more friendly they'd have strangled us.

They probably weren't space vampires either. Space vampires suck blood and, after all this ice-cream and almond tarts and curries and casseroles, none of this lot would be able to cram in even a little suck of jugular!

The ice-cream was good. Actually, anything would taste good after three months of spacegloop, but this was *really* good. It sort of melted on my tongue, so at first you only registered that it was cold, then the lovely creaminess spread all through my mouth and I got the first taste. Unlike artificial flavours that sort of hit you – pow! – and disappear except for chemical afterburn, real fruit tastes just go on and on and get better and better, till only a faint whiff is left on your tongue ...

I tried the passionfruit and found out what Dad meant about the taste of sunlight. Then I tried the chocolate and orange and was going to have a go at the lemon and coconut when someone pushed a glass of pineapple sorbet into one hand and these lacy biscuits to eat it with into the other.

This funny lady with a great wild mop of hair kept offering me peaches – tiny furry ones with red blotches like faint freckles that looked like the juice would spurt out as soon as your teeth plunged into it – though she could see I didn't have another hand to take one. Suddenly I knew that this was what fruit should smell like, even if I'd never breathed in anything like it before.

Well, I don't know how long we kept eating. I was feeling a bit sick, to tell you the truth – after three months of spacegloop my stomach wasn't used to proper food – but finally we staggered out (the peach lady insisted that I take some peaches with me, and someone had shoved a fat green watermelon into our luggage and a jar of chocolate pistachio biscuits) and the doors opened and ...

CHAPTER 8

... And it was *BIG!*

I knew what the outdoors looked like, no matter what Dad said. Back home, there was a four-hectare block of genuine 'outside' that they took us to in Geography class or on school excursions. But there's a real difference between seeing the wilderness for half an hour, with ultraviolet shielding all around you, and knowing you were going to live in it from now till ... *forever.* It just went on and on and on ...

The colours were too bright. Even the air was much too bright. I just couldn't take it all in. Then suddenly I blinked and everything sort of came together.

And I got my first breath of Callisto air.

It was terrifying. It was beautiful. It was just like Mum's window, but you could smell it and feel it on your skin.

It was like that fraction of a second after the rain before the smog rolls in again. It was like the best of Dad's soups you'd ever sniffed. It was like something I'd never smelt before but almost remembered. It was soft and warm and fruity and sweet and spicy.

I took a deeper breath. 'I'm going to like this place,' I said.

Dad was too busy grinning to even reply.

Fat little hovercars waited outside the terminal to take us where we needed to go, with the drivers sort of leaning against the cars and snacking on these great long rolls with the stuffing spilling out and passing punnets of squishy raspberries to each other and slices of watermelon from buckets filled with ice to keep the watermelon cold. One driver even had a big bowl of bean dip and crackers, which she offered to us in a friendly sort of fashion. She seemed disappointed when Dad said we were full.

'No charge, no charge,' she said when Dad asked how much the hovercraft ride would cost. 'We're a friendly lot here on Callisto 4. It's all part of the welcoming service.'

'Er ... thanks,' said Dad.

'Do you have far to go?'

Dad consulted his notes.

'Fullness of Heart, it says here,' he said. 'The third street from the crossing and the second house on the left.'

The bean dip woman nodded, as if those sort of directions were everyday to her. They probably were.

'Ah yes. Fullness of Heart is about two hours from here, just up from the Plenitude Sea. You'll love it there,' she said. 'Good peach country, with cherries on the rises and mangoes down in the subtropical dips by the sea. The best cream on the east coast too – oh, and the apricots! Wait till you taste the apricots! My daughter lives down that way. She and her husband have fifty-two varieties of apricots, and you should taste their blood oranges ...'

'You'll have to call in next time you're down that way,' said Dad expansively. 'We're going to run the café there, you know.'

The woman stared. 'The what?'

'The café,' repeated Dad. 'We swapped it ...'

The woman stared. And then she grinned. And then she started to laugh but turned it into a cough. The coughing fit went on and on.

'Hey, Saffron, are you all right?' one of the other drivers called out.

Our driver took a great gasping breath and nodded. 'It's just that they're going to run a café! A café on Callisto!'

The other driver moved closer and nudged her. 'Saffron, stop it! They're newcomers! What will they think of us!'

Our driver swallowed a final gurgle. 'I'm sorry. Just a tickle in my throat. Hop in, and I'll have you there by lunchtime.'

'Er ... thanks,' said Dad. We settled our luggage into the boot.

'It's probably the way we're dressed,' Dad whispered to me. 'We must look pretty drab and funny to Callisto natives.'

'Yeah, could be, Dad,' I said.

But I wasn't so sure.

What's so much fun
about starting again in a new place?

PART FOUR

CHAPTER 9

We spent the first day settling in. I had to admit it, Dad had been right.

Callisto looks as beautiful as it smells. There are no roads – just a few paths for pedestrians or bicycles, and the hovercraft wander through the forests. Where the forests end, the people have planted orchards of every kind of fruit tree you can imagine, all dripping cherries and apricots and the richest yellowest mangoes I'd ever seen. The soil is so fertile and the sun so gently constant that raspberries and strawberries just grow naturally about the trees, and every house looks almost smothered in flowers.

Only the hills are clear of vegetation, and that's where the animals graze. Callisto doesn't have much in the way of native animals; most of its native life is in the oceans, except for a few birds and things you need a microscope to see. So all the livestock are Earth species – velvety Jersey cows with big brown eyes, red and black hens that look like they're wearing long fluffy pants, long-necked geese that vanished from Earth so many years ago.

Everywhere you looked there were these great strong-looking people pruning fruit trees or harvesting huge baskets of corn. I couldn't even go for a walk down our road without someone racing over to the fence to offer me a nice squishy mango or a basket of fresh lychees or a case of ripe pineapples to take home to Dad. It took me a while to get used to treading on grass and flowers – tiny flowers bloom all through the grass on Callisto.

I was starting to understand why no one looked fat on Callisto – they were too busy growing food and cooking it and trying to get other people to eat it to put on weight themselves!

It was like something out of my picture books when I was a baby, about some fantasy life that people had lived two hundred years before. But this was true and real!

And everyone was so friendly. Incredible friendliness, the sort you never see on Earth nowadays. We hadn't been in the house ten minutes before someone came knocking.

'Yoo-hoo! It's only me!'

A face peered around the door. He was Dad's age, maybe, but with a sort of bright smock over even brighter trousers with birds embroidered all down the legs, just like the clothes we'd seen at the terminal.

I made myself a mental note that I'd need new clothes before I started school. As far as I was concerned, if the kids at school wore blue mud, then I'd wear blue mud too – or, in this case, bright clothes embroidered with birds and flowers. No way was I going to be more different than I had to be.

'I'm Herb from next door,' said the face. 'I just thought I'd pop in and welcome you to Callisto.'

Herb came in and set something wrapped in a steaming teatowel on the table. 'Just some homemade bread. It's my specialty. Stoneground flour from the plateau, then just a little olive oil and – this is the secret – finely ground macadamias!'

He'd just set the bread down on the table – and, before Dad could even say thank you or anything, someone else bustled through the doorway.

'Hello there! I see you're settling in. Good morning, Herb.' The newcomer didn't seem quite as keen to see Herb as she was to see us. She cast an annoyed glance down at the steaming fresh bread on the table. 'I'm Peaches Greenleaf from down the road and this is my husband, Radish,' she said, nodding her head at a broadly grinning man coming through the doorway.

Peaches had brought a goose and lentil casserole 'with apples and just a touch of nutmeg'. Her husband had brought a plate of lamingtons, and he sat there munching them while he told me and Dad all about his passionfruit vines and this really juicy apple variety he just happened to have twenty trees of, so anytime we felt like a few baskets of apples or a dozen pawpaws we only had to ask.

I pulled a hunk off the bread. It was soft and pale brown and doughy, and it steamed gently in my hand. I saw Peaches watching me, so I helped myself to some of her casserole too. She beamed at me kindly as I took my first mouthful.

'Er ... good!' I said. Her grin grew even wider. 'And the bread is great too!'

Herb beamed at me too. 'What a lovely daughter you have, Vince!' he said to Dad. 'So wonderfully intelligent for her age!'

'That's my Sam,' said Dad proudly. I took another mouthful of casserole and dipped the bread in the rich apple sauce. 'Mmmm,' I said.

Well, that was just the start.

By the end of the afternoon, the whole neighbourhood had dropped in and every one of them had brought a plate or jar or casserole of something to welcome us and I'd tried *everything* (just to be polite) and was trying not to burp in people's faces.

The fridge was full and the table creaked under its load, and there were tins of biscuits on every bench and baskets of rockmelons and great long carrots still with their ferny tops under the table too. The sink was full of beetroot and Dad was even forced to store a sack of potatoes (a special purple-skinned variety, really good for potato salads) in my bedroom.

'It's wonderful. Unbelievable,' Dad kept saying, rubbing a tomato – a real tomato – over and over in his hands like he was polishing it. 'Smell this! Just smell it! Genuine tomato! This is the life, eh, Sam?'

I nodded, my mouth full of peanut slice.

Dad rested his arms on the kitchen table, between a lamb and cauliflower casserole and a platter of chocolate fudge slices and apricot upside-down cake, and he gazed out the window. But this was a real window now that looked out onto the laden orange trees and the herb beds next door. (Our old window was still rolled up in our luggage.)

There were oranges *and* orange blossom on the tree at the same time, and I could smell both of them ... and peanut slice too.

'If only your Mum could have seen this,' Dad murmured. 'A café on Callisto. It's going to be paradise, Sam. Just paradise.'

I burped and bit into the coconutty chocolate fuzz around a lamington and tried to shush the mutterings in my mind.

CHAPTER 10

School was okay. I wore my new orange overalls with red and green apples embroidered down the front, bright blue sneakers and turquoise socks, and no one stared, so I reckon I looked pretty much like everyone else.

I guess school work is probably about the same anywhere in the universe. But the school itself was as different from my school back on Earth as Corridor 25 on Earth is from Blackberry Pie Street, Fullness of Heart.

First of all the school was big. There must have been at least 200 kids, maybe more! (Our corridor school cube had only seven kids, though of course all our lessons were vid-linked with every other kid in the country.) It took me days just to work out how to get around the school. Open spaces just aren't *logical* like corridors are.

The school itself was a long building, shaped like a lazy snake, that wandered in and out of gardens that no one ever seemed to tend, with geese to keep the grass down (and pinch your lunch if you didn't watch out) and eat the fallen apples and apricots and avocados as they plopped off the fruit trees planted around the school and sometimes munch a few flowers for dessert.

Sometimes it was hard to concentrate in maths – actually it's always hard to concentrate in maths – what with the thud of ripe fruit on the grass and the scent of flowers so thick you could almost slice it and the *twitter twitter pobble pobble* of all the bright birds in the trees.

I'd never realised that fruit has so many smells before – one smell when it's on the tree, a hot dirt and warm fruit smell when it's on the ground, a ginger beer and almost clean garbage bin smell when it starts to rot and yet another scent when it's all cut up and chilled from the fridge.

What was I saying? Oh, the birds. I never knew there were so many birds in the universe either! They were a zillion bright colours, just like the people's clothes, and they were fat!

The birds were native to Callisto, unlike the geese. They were fruit eaters and it seemed as if they had just been waiting for humans to move in and start planting more fruit trees so they could start gutsing.

Native Callisto fruits are pretty small by comparison, and those birds must have thought they were in paradise when they first discovered Earth fruit.

'They're called pobble-pobble birds,' said Cherry, who sat next to me in class. 'You get great flocks of them sometimes – hundreds and hundreds. They move around, depending on what's ripe. Sometimes you can hardly see the trees, there are so many pobble-pobbles in them.'

'Don't the pobble-pobbles damage the fruit trees?' I asked.

'Nah.' Cherry opened a date and banana sandwich, inspected it, then threw it to one of the geese. The goose pecked it halfheartedly. The geese were so fat they could hardly waddle. 'There's more than enough fruit for everyone.'

Cherry unwrapped a tiny quiche, sniffed it, then offered it to me. 'Want one?'

'Hey, thanks.'

'Don't thank me. I'm sick of them. Mum's always making quiches. It's her specialty. Chicken quiche, spinach quiche, mushroom and almond quiche ...'

'Dad cooks too. That's why we came here. Dad's going to reopen the café ...'

Cherry blinked. 'What's a café?'

'Huh? A café's where you go to buy meals.'

'Oh sure. Now I remember,' said Cherry vaguely. 'They've got cafés on Earth, haven't they? I read about them in geography.' She sounded totally uninterested.

'They've got cafés on other places.'

'Not on Callisto,' said Cherry.

'No, Callisto's only got one. We swapped it for our café on Earth and ...'

'I never knew we had a café here!'

'But ...' I hesitated. Surely the café had been open before? I mean, it was there, with tables and everything. How come Cherry had never heard of it?

'I suppose you like cooking too,' said Cherry disgustedly. She threw another crust to the goose.

'Not much. I really like eating though.'

'You don't like cooking!' Cherry's face lit up. 'Wow! Neither do I! Hey, do you want to come over to my place sometime? I'm building a go-cart.'

'Sure.'

Cherry bit into an apple thoughtfully. 'I'm *really* glad you don't like cooking. You've no idea how boring it gets around here.'

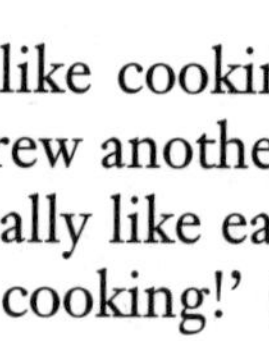

CHAPTER 11

Cherry asked me to dinner at her place the first weekend I was there.

'Mum says I have to,' she explained glumly.

I blinked. 'Don't you want me to come over to your place?'

'Sure,' said Cherry. 'You're totally supanova great! But dinner!'

'What wrong with dinner?'

Cherry sniffed. 'Just don't feel you have to eat everything to be polite. Especially not Mum's quiches. You're not family or anything, so you don't have to eat anything you don't want to!'

'Yeah okay,' I said, bewildered. It was going to take a while to find my feet.

Cherry's house was supanova sensational. It was almost as long as our school and built out of real wood too. It sort of wandered along by a creek with all these deep rocky pools and splashy little waterfalls where you could swim all day, except when you were making a go-cart or a cubby among the fruit trees, and when you were hungry you just had to swim up to the bank and pick a few squishy fat blueberries from the bushes that grew along the bank.

Cherry's dad and mum and baby sister lived in one part of the house and her grandparents lived in another, and somewhere a few aunts and uncles fitted in too. But, like I said, there was plenty of room.

There was plenty of food too.

'Have another apple tart, Samdolyn dear!' insisted Cherry's mum.

'Mum! She's already had four!' wailed Cherry.

'I'm sure she can fit in just one more.'

'Er ... I'm sort of full of pumpkin soup spinach quiche roast chicken roast goose bean and sausage casserole corn on the cob potato bake stir-fried cauliflower steamed snow peas stuffed cabbage stuffed tomatoes carrot surprise buttered noodles cheesecake lemon meringue sticky-date pudding and an apple. But thank you anyway,' I said politely.

'Maybe just a slice of pineapple upside-down cake then,' offered Cherry's Auntie Apricot. 'With my special vanilla custard sauce.'

'Auntie Apricot!' hissed Cherry 'You are so embarrassing!'

'Nonsense,' beamed Auntie Apricot. 'Children on Earth hardly get anything to eat. Isn't that right, Samdolyn?'

'Er, sort of,' I said. 'Not food like this anyway. But my Dad's a cook, so I ate pretty well. He's going to open a café here.'

'A what?' demanded Cherry's great-grandmother. 'Speak up, girl! I can't hear you!'

'A café,' I yelled down the table.

'She said "a café", mother!' yelled Cherry's dad even louder. He hadn't eaten much during dinner. His plate was still piled almost as high as it was when we'd started eating. He was really skinny and had a sort of grey indigestion look about him too.

'A café! A café on Callisto! Oh dear! Oh dear, oh dear, oh dear!' Cherry's great-grandmother started laughing so hard she choked on her cherry and cream cheese strudel with walnut ice-cream, and had to be helped from the table.

I was definitely getting the feeling Dad and I might be in trouble.

CHAPTER 12

By the end of our second week Dad was ready to reopen the café.

There were blue and white checked cloths on the tables (the previous owner had left them, along with most of the other café equipment), a pineapple pizza in the oven and genuine tomato soup simmering on the stove. There were chocolate cheesecakes on the dessert tray and passionfruit mousse in the fridge. (We finally had to throw out most of the stuff the neighbours had left – it was all really good but, after all, how much can two people eat?) Dad had programmed the music – soft happy stuff so people could still talk without it banging in their ears.

Cherry and I'd made this supanova-sized banner which said 'Grand Opening'. Well, actually, it said 'Grand Oppening'. Spelling isn't my strong point.

'Don't worry about it,' said Cherry, as she helped me string it up over the front door. 'A man on a galloping horse would never notice it. It looks nice and bright, anyway.'

She stood back to admire it. 'Wow. This is really exciting. I never thought I'd see a real café in my life!' She made it sound as if a café was a tyrannosaurus or something totally weird.

'Do you want to stay for the opening?'

Cherry shook her head. 'I'd like to, but we've got to go over to Auntie Lamington's for dinner. She gets really miffed if we don't turn up – she says that, after all, she comes over to our place for Mum's quiches every second Tuesday, the least we can do is come and eat her sausages. She makes them with chopped chicken and veal and I don't know what, but I bet she'll tell me again anyway.'

'Cherry,' I said slowly. 'Do you really think ...?'

'Hey, girls! Come and help me with the flowers!' yelled Dad.

About ninety of our ultrafriendly neighbours had left about a hundred and sixty great bucketloads of flowers all crawling with bees and butterflies as soon as they heard that Dad might like a few flowers. There were roses and ... and ... and lots of other flowers that I don't know the names of and probably never will because – who cares about flower names? They still look pretty and smell good no matter what they're called.

By the time we'd finished turning them into posies for each table, it was late and Cherry had to go.

So we opened the café.

The first hour Dad kept the tomato soup simmering, stirring it and waiting for me to bring in the first order.

The second hour he let it cool, and chopped stuff for the next day.

The third hour he turned off the kitchen light, took off his chef's hat and sat with me on the doorstep.

I could have told Dad what was going to happen. On a planet like Callisto, who's going to want to come to a café? Why buy food when everyone you meet wants you to try something for free? Not just wants to, mind you, but practically stuffs it down your throat.

This was worse than flesh-eating slime and volcanoes. It was even worse than space vampires. At least Dad could have sold them blood puddings.

We watched the moon slowly bob over the horizon, the oranges on the trees next door glowing softly in the light and the smell of roses and chocolate cheesecake and real tomato soup all around us. Even if there weren't any customers, it was sort of peaceful.

I thought, 'Mum would have liked this,' and my throat sort of choked for a minute.

'I should have known,' said Dad finally. 'I did know in my heart. As soon as we got here really. I just didn't want to face it.'

'Maybe you can do something else?' I offered.

Dad shrugged. 'What? I've always been a cook and run a café. I've never wanted to do anything else. Those are the only two things I know how to do – and they are the two things no one really needs out here.'

'Maybe ...' I said slowly. Well, to tell the truth, I don't know what I was going to say. I was just hoping some words would sort of float into my mouth, when suddenly a small hovercraft fluttered between the trees, and someone got out.

For a moment, in the darkness, it was hard to tell if the person was male or female. Then the figure moved up into the light by the door and I could see.

It was a woman, but she was the largest woman I'd ever seen. Not that she was fat; don't get me wrong. She was just *big*, even bigger than just about anyone else I'd seen on Callisto. She was well over two metres high, with shoulders as wide as the door and lots of long brown hair, and she moved as if she could pick up our whole café and just stroll off with it.

'Evening,' she said softly (her voice seemed too soft for someone so large, but it was sort of nice). 'Is this the café?'

Dad didn't say anything. Maybe he was shocked at a female giant appearing out of nowhere, or maybe he was too depressed.

'Sure,' I said.

The giant grinned. Her overalls were bright pink, with purple butterflies embroidered along the front – typical Callisto clothes. 'Well, I'm a customer, so if you'd just move off the steps a bit ...'

Dad looked up at that. 'A customer? Here on Callisto?'

She nodded. Her long hair bobbed against her shoulders.

'A real customer?'

The giant looked down at herself, all twenty hectares of pink overalls and purple butterflies, then back at Dad. 'Well, I'm a bit too substantial not to be real.'

Dad got to his feet. Dad isn't a small man, but he looked tiny next to the giant. 'How come?' he demanded. 'Are you the only person on Callisto who doesn't like cooking?'

The giant grinned again, showing lots of big white teeth. 'Well, there are a few of us who don't like to cook. Not many, I have to admit.'

'Then why don't you let someone else feed you?' I asked. 'Why do you want to go and buy a meal?'

The giant shrugged. 'If you accept a meal from someone, you have to say it's good. And if you say it's good, they'll want to feed you again and again ... and then you'll offend everyone else who wants you to try their blueberry muffins or their apple and date pies. So, tonight I'm not going to offend anyone. I'm coming here.'

She was almost laughing now. 'If you'll just move out of the way so I can come in ...'

The giant – her name was Rosemary – ate three helpings of Dad's spaghetti with pine nuts and garlic, then she asked me if I'd like to sit with her while she ate a piece of coconut peach cake and walnut ice-cream.

'You want some too?' she asked.

I hesitated. 'I already ate out in the kitchen. But I'll eat some to keep you company.'

So we each had another bowl of ice-cream. I'd never seen anyone eat as much as Rosemary. It wasn't that she ate fast or greedily, she just ate efficiently – one spoonful after another after another ...

'It's because I'm so big,' she explained, swishing her long brown hair out of the way so she could attack her ice-cream more efficiently. 'When you're my size you need a lot of fuel. Plus I use up a lot of energy in my job. You know, this is fantastic ice-cream.'

'What do you do?'

'I build houses. I really build them – design them and draw up the plans, then put up the structures. I even do the finishing too – make the kitchen benches and window frames. I like to do a bit of everything.'

'That sounds like the best job in the world!'

She looked up from her ice-cream. 'I would have thought you'd like cooking, like your Dad?'

'I'd rather eat,' I said. 'I like seeing how things are made. Wow, you mean you start with nothing at all and then the house just grows around you?'

I'd never met anyone who built houses before. I'd read about it, but no one on Earth even lived in a house any more – just the underground complexes away from the UV and the factory pollution up top. Rosemary was the first person I'd met who really knew *how* to build something, not just how to fiddle around with prefab sheets of plastic.

'You want to come out to a building site sometime?' asked Rosemary, wiping her mouth with her napkin and glancing back at the dessert trolley.

'Hey, wow, can I really? That would be totally supanova fabulous!' I followed her glance. 'Would you like some more dessert? A piece of pie?'

'No thanks.'

There was a silence for a moment, as though she expected me to say something, then she said, 'You're not going to try to persuade me to have the pie?'

'No, of course not,' I said, offended. 'It's bad manners to try to persuade a customer to have something they don't really want.'

Rosemary burst out laughing again. She had a big laugh, bigger than you'd think with her soft voice. 'You know, this must be the only place on Callisto where if you eat something you're not expected to eat some more!'

Rosemary paid her bill – I think Dad would have insisted she eat for nothing, as our first customer, but I nudged him. We did have to make a living and, anyway, that's why Rosemary had come to the café – to actually buy food instead of feeling obligated, and I was afraid that if Dad didn't let her pay she mightn't come back.

'She was nice,' I said to Dad after she left.

Dad stared out the door as Rosemary's hovercraft lifted above the orange trees. He nodded vaguely. He still seemed sort of dazed.

Maybe it was just Rosemary's size or her appetite, or maybe something else.

'Well at least we had one customer,' I said, as Dad turned off the lights. 'I bet she'll come back too.'

Dad looked out the window again at where Rosemary's hovercraft had sat. 'One customer isn't going to make a living for us,' he warned.

I nodded. But things seemed brighter since Rosemary's visit.

CHAPTER 13

Rosemary came to dinner at the café the following night, and the next. Dad made chicken and leek pie with a shiny flaky top and stuffed meatballs in genuine Callisto tomato sauce and peach and turkey kebabs that smelt of lemon thyme and lots of garlic. Rosemary ate three helpings of everything and settled down to dessert.

I kept hoping that maybe Rosemary would bring a friend or two who didn't like cooking either, but they must have been busy being stuffed by their aunties or someone.

The next day was Saturday, and Rosemary had to go to her second cousin's birthday party. But Dad kept the café open anyway.

He sort of mooched around the kitchen, rolling out puff pastry that no one was going to eat, and I mooched around the café, putting fresh flowers on the tables and folding the napkins into the shape of swans (I thought it'd impress Rosemary when she came on Monday).

I'd just finished the last swan when Cherry came in.

'Hi,' I said.

'Hi.' She looked around curiously. 'Where are all the customers? I thought cafés always had lots of people sitting at the tables. That's what it says in the geography book.'

'Well, they don't always,' I said. Not on Callisto anyway, I thought, but I didn't say it. I didn't want Cherry to think I didn't like her planet. And I did like it! I loved Callisto. I just wished there was some way Dad could make a living here too.

Cherry just nodded. I suppose she thought I was an expert on cafés. 'I brought the maths homework over so we could do it together.'

I nodded gratefully. They were doing stuff that was new to me and it was going to take a while for me to catch up. 'I'll just get my homework book.' (We used real books with pages and covers and *pens* on Callisto – totally antique! But you get used to anything, I guess.)

'Okay.' Cherry sat down. She looked at me, sort of puzzled.

'Cherry? What's wrong?'

Cherry shrugged, then she grinned. ‘You haven’t offered me anything to eat yet. It’s what always happens on Callisto. As soon as you go to someone’s place and sit down, they start dragging out the cakes and biscuits and their great-grandmother’s recipe for lemon cordial ...’

‘Well, you can have something to eat if you want to,’ I said. I wanted to fit in. I gestured at the menu. ‘Choose anything you like! Pineapple pizza. Or the pineapple frangipani tart is really good. So’s the blueberry ice-cream.’

Cherry gave it a glance, then looked at it more closely. ‘What are all those numbers?’

‘They’re prices.’

‘Prices?’

‘That’s what you pay for the food.’

Cherry blinked. ‘You mean in a café you have to pay to eat?’

‘Yeah, sure. But *you* don’t have to, of course, because you’re a friend.’

‘What if people don’t pay?’

I stared. 'Well, then they don't get anything to eat.'

Cherry looked as if she'd just seen a giant Christmas tree with every present carrying her name. 'You mean, if I come here and I don't pay anything, I don't have to eat anything? Nothing at all! No one would give me *anything* to eat?'

'I suppose so. But ...'

Cherry's face was glowing. 'Oh wow! Oh wow! Wait till I tell Dad. Do you mind if I bring Dad here?'

'Yes, I mean no, but ...'

'Dad's like me,' explained Cherry. 'He's just not keen on food. And Auntie Applecake too – she was saying just the other day she wished there was *some* place she could go and chat with her friends without being forced to be polite and eat and ...'

We never did get our homework done that day.

CHAPTER 14

Well, that's the end of the story because I suppose you can guess what happened then.

Cherry brought her Dad over the next afternoon, and he just sat there yarning with us and not eating *anything*. And the next day after work he brought a couple of his mates with him.

It turned out they were sick of eating too. All they wanted to do was sit and talk for a while, with no one offering them plates of crisp sunflower and almond bread or moist rich carrot cake ...

Then Cherry's Aunt Applecake brought all her friends along, and they happily didn't eat anything either. And all the teachers from school came for their end-of-year dinner, except without the dinner.

It seems that every year the teachers all argued and argued about who'd be the lucky one to feed them all, so this year they decided to come to us! Plus *not* eating at our place meant they'd still be empty enough to eat at home!

The new sign that Cherry and I made was even brighter than the first one – and this time we spelt it right. 'Café Callisto – you only have to eat here if you buy our food! (Cover charge, 50 barterdollars)'

By the following Saturday the café was full!

'It's wonderful, Sam! Simply wonderful!' Dad kept saying as we sat at the counter and polished the glasses and water jugs.

I gazed out over all our delighted customers, sitting at our tables with my flower decorations and the swan-shaped napkins, listening to Dad's soft happy-making music and gossiping with their friends ... and eating absolutely nothing at all.

'We're going to be rich, Dad!' I informed him. 'In fact, I think we need to open a chain of cafés. We can call them ... Dad? Dad, are you listening?'

'What? Oh yes, yes of course, Sam,' said Dad vaguely, his eyes on the doorway. Another customer had just come in, and if the place had looked packed before it looked even fuller with her in it.

'Hi, Rosemary!' I yelled.

Rosemary made her way between the crowded tables over to the counter. 'I knew you'd be a success!' she beamed.

‘Yeah!’ I said. ‘And Dad’s made these really supanova delicious lamb and artichoke kebabs especially for you, and there’s corn on the cob and stir-fried beans with mushrooms and potato casserole plus your favourite ice-cream and ...’

I stopped. For once Rosemary didn’t seem so interested in the menu. She was looking at Dad and Dad was looking at her and ...

Well, you don’t have to hit me on the head with a case of ripe pineapples for me to get the message.

‘I’ll just go and dish it up, will I?’ I asked, and left them to it.

And that seemed to be the end of that story too. Or maybe just the beginning ...

Well, anyway, Dad and I are making a mint! Everybody comes here when they don’t want to eat and even on Callisto there are times when people don’t want to munch on anything, so our café’s always full.

Dad has finally started thinking about my idea of opening a chain of cafés right across Callisto too, though he’s a bit worried they might lose the personal touch that ours has now.

Like Dad always said, it's not just the food that makes a café. Our café has the most sparkling water jugs on the whole of Callisto, the brightest tablecloths, the cutest posies on the tables and the happiest background music. Dad's put in racks of books and magazines too, so people can just sit quietly by themselves and not be interrupted halfway through a really great story by someone trying to get them to eat some fabulous variety of juicy peach or a dozen slices of pawpaw marinated in orange juice with just a touch of black pepper.

Dad mightn't be the absolute best cook on Callisto (though Rosemary and I think he's pretty close), but he *doesn't* cook better than anyone!

Of course, Dad doesn't get to prepare food for customers any more, but he gets to cook for Rosemary instead, and now that they're married and I help Rosemary after school and during school holidays, I'm eating more than ever too.

Rosemary says, she and I are going into partnership as soon as I leave school. We're going to call ourselves 'Rosemary Victor and

Stepdaughter, Architects and Builders'. Or maybe it'll just be 'Rosemary and Sam: we build it; you live in it'.

There is nothing like nailing up roof trusses with Rosemary to give you an appetite for Dad's deep dish tomato and meatball pizza with lots of lettuce, cucumber and avocado salad with chopped parsley, and chocolate raspberry doughnuts for dessert, and Cherry thinks so too.

I reckon I'm like a Callisto tomato now, full of sun and fresh air and spreading my leaves all over the place.

Dad was right. Callisto tomatoes aren't like the ones on Earth. And cafés just aren't the same either.